Traction Man

AND THE

Beach Odyssey

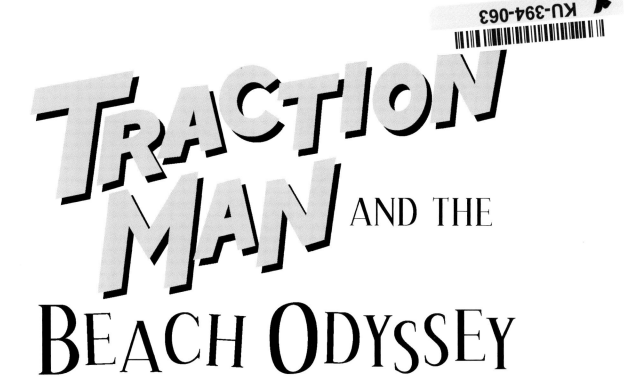

Mini Grey

JONATHAN CAPE
London

Scrubbing Brush has never been on holiday before and is quite excited.

Granny's coming too. She has a new Young Pet called Truffles.

Scrubbing Brush thinks Truffles needs some Proper Training . . .

My goodness! Look at that —
it must be the Wide Ocean!

BIG AND SPARKLY

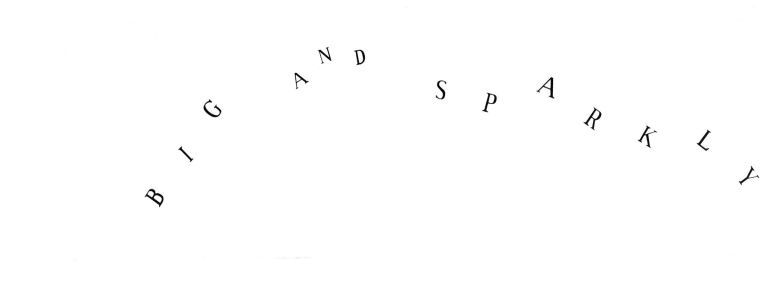

FISHSTICKS
COD 'N' HALIBUT FLAVOUR

Traction Man and Scrubbing Brush
are exploring the secret crevices of the Rockpool.

Traction Man is wearing his Squid-Proof Scuba Suit,
Lightweight Shorts and Aquatic Air Tanks.

Who knows what creatures lurk
in this Underwater World?

If they stay very still
perhaps some of the
elusive Rockpool Animals
will appear.

Nearly everyone wanted to have a quick dip in the sea before lunch –

which leaves Traction Man and Scrubbing Brush and . . .

OPERATION PICNIC.

At all costs, this picnic must be defended against hungry Truffles.

DIG
DIG
DIG

But Truffles must think Traction Man is some sort of bone and has carried him off.

Oh no! Traction Man has been buried for later.

Don't worry Traction Man, Scrubbing Brush has sturdy bristles and will dig you out in a jiffy.

Traction Man and Scrubbing Brush
are clinging onto a plastic bottle
in the vast sea.
They can hardly see land.

A colossal wave
towers
over them.

Traction Man is wearing
quite a lot of seaweed.

It's all dark.

Scrubbing Brush,
where are you?

Arf!

Thank
goodness!

Can you see that shape
in the gloom?

Keep very still Scrubbing Brush,
and don't be scared
(even though it has
hot breath
and dripping jaws).

But do you hear a voice?

What have you got there, Fluffy?

Traction Man and Scrubbing Brush are travelling by bucket . . .

Beach-Time Brenda™ Bucket

Well, we'll be going soon - but maybe he's been washed up further along...

Traction Man is in the Dollies' Castle, wearing seaweed
hair and beard, a shell hat, a light dusting of sand
and a floral sarong.
Scrubbing Brush has been garlanded too.
The Dollies are treating them to a feast of ice-cream
and lollies.

. . . about this long, wearing a red scuba suit . . .

SNUFFLE SNUFFLE

Look there, Scrubbing Brush —
do you recognise that nose?

I'm afraid your castle has been demolished
by Truffles the Puppy.
But don't worry, Traction Man and Scrubbing
Brush can help you rebuild it in no time.

Traction Man, Scrubbing Brush and the Dollies
are digging an exploration hole
to the Centre of the Earth.

(The Dollies are wearing Safety Jackets,
Excavation Shorts and Cave Helmets
borrowed from Traction Man.)

They have already unearthed
these buried treasures and the bones
of some ancient creature.

Behind them you can see
the Dollies' new castle.
They think it is Even Better than before.

Tomorrow they are all going to go
on an expedition to the Mysterious Cave
with their own lunch.

The Dollies have a dinghy . . .
and they are all
ready for
Anything.

Some other brilliant books by Mini Grey:

Egg Drop
The Pea and the Princess
Biscuit Bear
Traction Man Is Here
The Adventures of the Dish and the Spoon
Traction Man Meets Turbodog
Jim (by Hilaire Belloc, illustrated by Mini Grey)
Three by the Sea

HOOH
ingeniously made of potato

Dedicated
to
TIA

TRACTION MAN AND THE BEACH ODYSSEY
A JONATHAN CAPE BOOK 978 0 224 08364 5

Published in Great Britain by Jonathan Cape,
an imprint of Random House Children's Books
A Random House Group Company

This edition published 2011

3 5 7 9 10 8 6 4 2

Copyright © Mini Grey, 2011

The right of Mini Grey to be identified as the author of this work has
been asserted in accordance with the Copyright, Designs and Patents Act 1988.

RANDOM HOUSE CHILDREN'S BOOKS
www.kidsatrandomhouse.co.uk

Addresses for companies within The Random House Group Limited can be found at:
www.randomhouse.co.uk/offices.htm

RANDOM HOUSE BOOKS 61-63 Uxbridge Road, London W5 5SA

THE RANDOM HOUSE GROUP Limited Rep. No. 954009

A CIP catalogue record for this book is available from the British Library.

Printed in Singapore

Fully Posable Brenda

fluttering eyelashes

nodding head

realistic hair

twistable limbs

unrealistic Vital Statistics

essential phone

small plastic barbecue

pinkly paisley inflatable dinghy

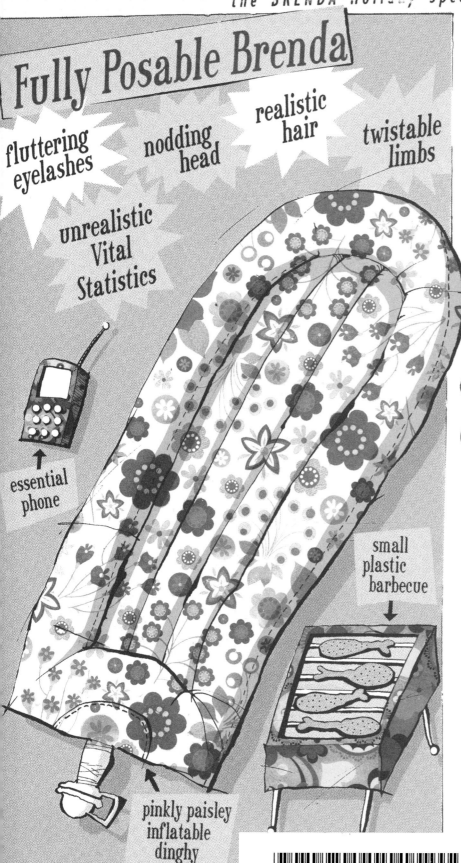

APPLY. NON-WATERPROOF – MAY DISINTEGRATE I... ...SUN. WARNING: CHOKING HAZARD AND SMALL PARTS.